BOTTLES BREAK

Nancy María Grande Tabor

ini Charlesbridge

Para Jorge
And in memory of Don

Published by Charlesbridge Publishing
85 Main Street, Watertown, MA 02472
(617) 926-0329

Library of Congress Cataloging-in-Publication Data
Tabor, Nancy.
Bottles break/Nancy María Grande Tabor.
p.   cm.
Summary: A child describes how it feels when a parent drinks.
ISBN 0-88106-317-7 (reinforced for library use)
ISBN 0-88106-318-5 (softcover)
[1. Alcoholism—Fiction. 2. Parent and child—Fiction.]
I. Title.
PZ7.T1145Bo   1999
[E]—dc21   97-15197

Printed in the United States of America
(hc) 10 9 8 7 6 5 4 3 2 1
(sc) 10 9 8 7 6 5 4 3 2 1

The illustrations in this book were done in tissue paper
on construction paper and were modified in Adobe Photoshop.
The display type and text type were set in Tiepolo and Lemonade.
Color separations were made by Eastern Rainbow, Derry, New Hampshire.
Printed and bound by Worzalla Publishing Company, Stevens Point, Wisconsin
Production supervision by Brian G. Walker
Designed by Diane M. Earley
This book was printed on recycled paper.

That is me.
That little speck.
That is what I feel like.
I feel very small and like I do not count.

These are bottles.
Lots of bottles all over the place.
My mom leaves bottles all over the place.

Sometimes I find them under the bed.
Sometimes in a corner.
Sometimes on the living room floor.

This is a bottle.
Some people think bottles are beautiful.
Some people would give their whole life for a bottle

Sometimes I think my mom would rather have a bottle than me.

Bottles come in many shapes and colors,

and so do the people who drink from them.

But inside the many different bottles
is the same thing—ALCOHOL.

And inside the *many* different people is the same thing, too—a *desire* for alcohol.

These are lots of bottles. First they are full . . .

then they are empty. No one wants empty
bottles, so people just leave them around.

The people who drink from these bottles are just like the bottles. Before they drink, they are full. They count as people.

But after they drink, they seem empty.

You cannot talk to them because they do not understand. They act a little strange and do silly or terrible things.

Sometimes they get mad and angry,
and they scream and shout.
Sometimes they cry.

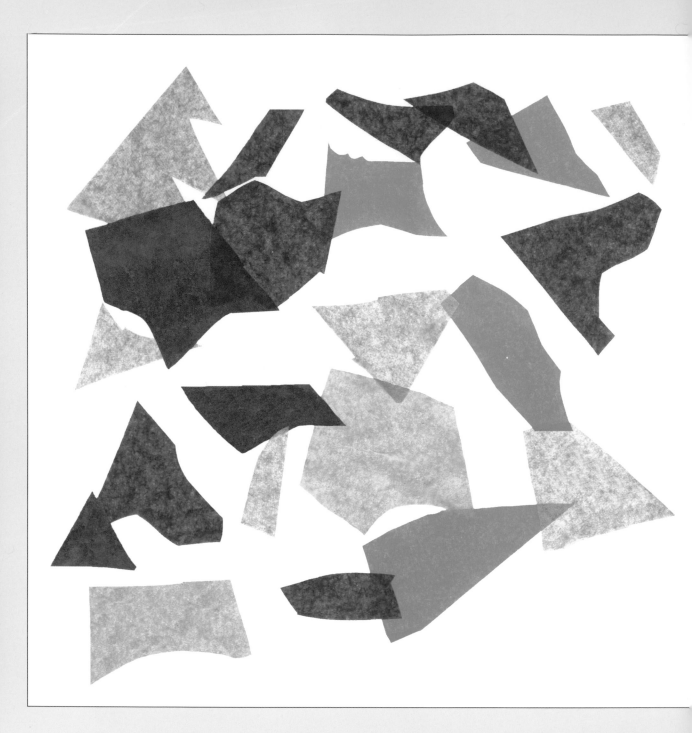

Sometimes they throw the bottles, and the bottles break. Empty, broken bottles can hurt, and so can empty, broken people.

I hurt, and I know my mom does, too.
I see her crying and falling apart.

I can throw the empty, broken bottles away.
I can sweep them out of the house.
But not my mom.

I want my mom to stay with me.
I want it to be me and my mom.
But NO BOTTLES.

Why do people drink?

why does it hurt so much?

Is it my fault?

Did I do something bad?

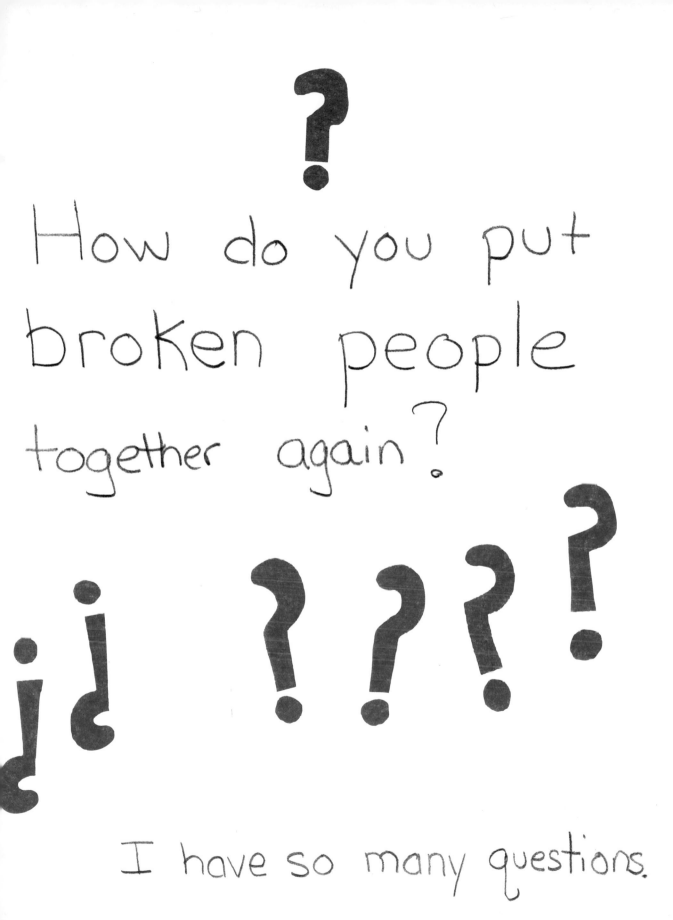

My teacher saw what I wrote, and she asked me if I wanted to talk about it.

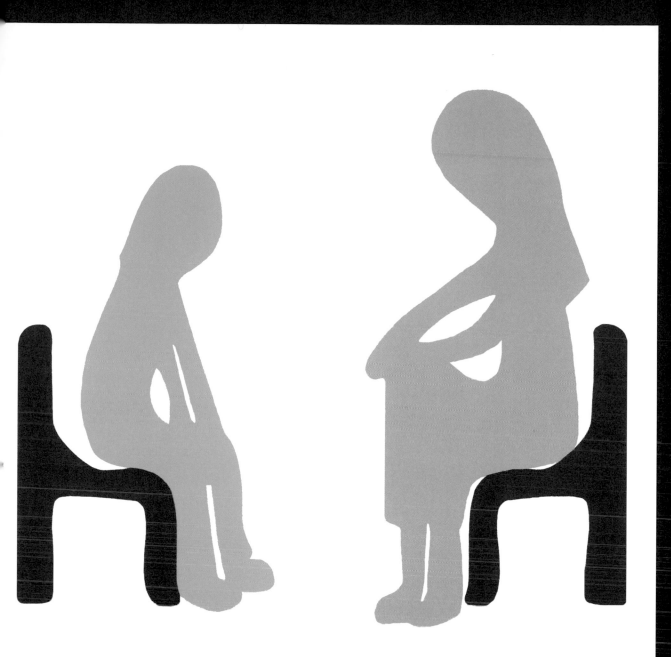

She told me to try not to feel bad
and that *my mom's* drinking is not *my* fault.
he said *my mom* has a disease called alcoholism.

She said that when I am feeling bad about
my mom, I can do things like ride my bike,
read a book,

play with my friends, or write.

Some days my mom plays with me or walks with me, reads with me or talks with me.

I wish I could enjoy
being with *my mom* every day.

But when she drinks,
I do things that make me feel better.

This is me.
ow I do not feel like that little speck anymore.
I am getting bigger and bigger every day.

If a parent or someone close to you drinks,
here are some places to contact for help and information:

a trusted family member or friend
a school nurse
a guidance counselor
a religious organization
a teacher

Al-Anon or Alateen
1600 Corporate Landing Parkway
Virginia Beach, VA 23454
(800) 356-9996 or (800) 344-2666
(757) 563-1600 (family group headquarters) • www.al-anon.alateen.org

National Association for Children of Alcoholics
11426 Rockville Pike, Suite 100
Rockville, MD 20852
(888) 554-COAS(2627) • www.health.org/nacoa
(The web site includes a section just for children.)

National Council on Alcoholism and Drug Dependence, Inc.
12 West 21st Street
New York, NY 10010
(800) NCA-CALL (622-2255) • (212) 206-6770 • www.ncadd.org

National Clearinghouse for Alcohol and Drug Information
maintains a web site for children at www.health.org/kidsarea

American Academy of Child and Adolescent Psychiatry
provides information about children of alcoholics at
www.aacap.org/factsfam/alcoholc.htm

Remember, 800 and 888 numbers are toll-free. Don't forget to dial 1 first.
At the time of publication, all WWW addresses were correct and operational.